A Crazy-much LOVE

BY
Joy Jordan-Lake

two lions

ILLUSTRATED BY
Sonia Sánchez

For Jasmine,
whom we love forever and ever and far beyond that;

and for Chloe, EB, Grace Ann, Gracie, Josie, Kendyl, Kylie,
Lucy, and Steffi, who, along with their parents and siblings,
have become a cherished part of our own family;

and for Kenbe, who is strong and fun and fabulous;

and for everyone who has experienced the extraordinary gift
of adoption: *May your life's journey be one of crazy-much love.*
–J. J-L.

For my crazy love Alejandro
–S. S.

Published by Two Lions, New York • www.apub.com
Amazon, the Amazon logo, and Two Lions are trademarks of
Amazon.com, Inc., or its affiliates.

ISBN-13: 9781542043267 • ISBN-10: 1542043263
The illustrations are rendered in digital media.
Book design by Abby Dening

Printed in China
First Edition
1 3 5 7 9 10 8 6 4 2

You are the one,
precious child—
did you know?

We dreamed about you
and pictured you waiting for us . . .

just like we were
waiting for you.

We loved you before we saw you,
or hugged you,
or held you.

You were the one
we hoped for,
and prayed for,

and piled up stuffed bears for.

It was you.

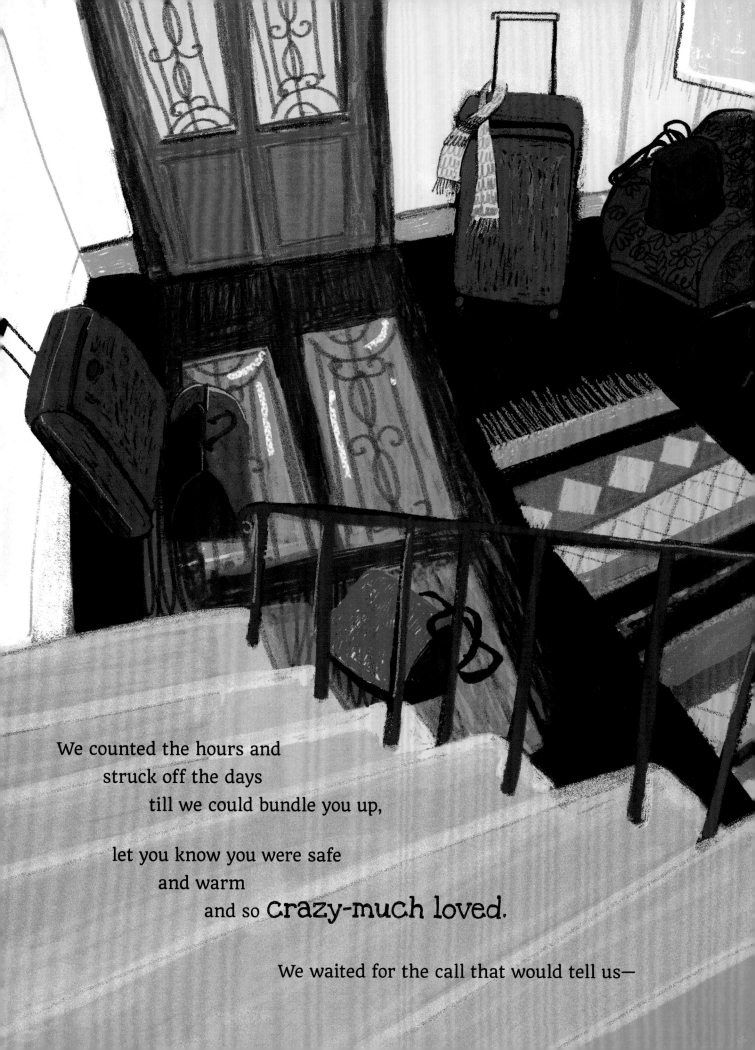

We counted the hours and
struck off the days
till we could bundle you up,

let you know you were safe
and warm
and so **crazy-much loved.**

We waited for the call that would tell us—

it was time AT LONG LAST to meet you.

And when our waiting was over,
we traveled to you in a

big,

crazy

rush,

never stopping . . .

until you were snuggled up
safe in our arms.

We told you we'd love you

**forever and ever
and far beyond that,**

and you looked
into our eyes like you felt it
right down to your toes.

It was you.

We brought you home,

where a **crazy-loud family** was pacing the floor
and waiting
        to celebrate YOU.

When you arrived

everyone CHEERED...

and the dog licked your toes—
your very first laugh!

And we knew—

our **crazy-much love** for you
would grow
and grow more

**and spill out the windows
and bust down the doors.**

It was you.

When you had your first bath,
bubbles up to your chin,

and you clapped your hands in delight,
foam flying high,
and turned the dog fluffy white.

When you took your first steps
and walked into our arms.

And our arms were so
crazy-much full.

When you said your first word . . .

"WOOF!"

And your first sentence
shouted so loud,
both your arms overhead.

"I love you MUCH!"

We answered back,

"Forever and ever and far beyond that!"

It was you.

When you rode your first trike
so fast you sailed off the path,
but then you popped up with your dimples and grin.

When you boarded the big yellow bus for the first time,

and we waved
and we cried with joy
for how crazy-well
you had grown.

And then just as the doors shut . . .

the dog's nose poked out of your pack!

All those times and ALWAYS, we knew.

It was you.

And now, at night,
when you nestle deep into bed
and ask from under the quilt,

"HOW MUCH is the crazy-much love?"

we hug you tighter than tight
and say,

"SO MUCH that it
    spills out the windows
        and busts down the doors."

And then you ask,

"HOW LONG does it last,
the crazy-much love?"

You laugh
    because you already know.

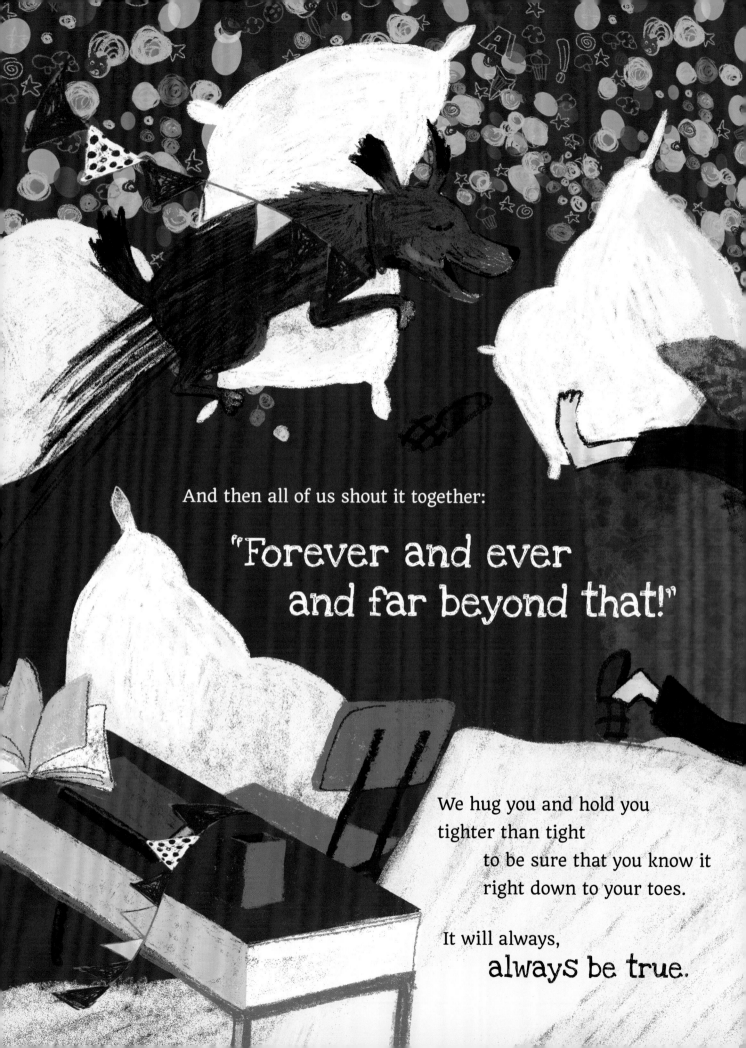

And then all of us shout it together:

"Forever and ever
and far beyond that!"

We hug you and hold you
tighter than tight
        to be sure that you know it
        right down to your toes.

It will always,
        always be true.

We've been given
the greatest of
crazy-much gifts.

It is YOU.